BEASTLY BEHAVIORS

FIND THE BAFFLING BONDS BETWEEN AMAZING ANIMALS

Written by Jeff O'Hare

Illustrated by Marc Nadel

Boyds Mills Press

This one's for Edward–the King of the Jungle
Love, Dad

For Nancy and James with much love
—Marc

Special thanks to the staff at the Zoological Society of San Diego:
Don Boyer, Curator of Reptiles and Amphibians
Karen Killmar, Associate Curator of Mammals
Ed Lewins, Curator of Birds
Valerie Thompson, Associate Curator of Mammals
Georgeanne Irvine, Communications Manager, Development

Published by Boyds Mills Press, Inc.
A Highlights Company
815 Church Street
Honesdale, Pennsylvania 18431
Printed in China
Visit our Web site at www.boydsmillspress.com

U.S. Cataloging-in-Publication Data
(Library of Congress Standards)

O'Hare, Jeff.
Beastly behaviors : find the baffling bonds between amazing animals /
by Jeff O'Hare ; illustrated by Marc Nadel.—1st ed.
[32] p. : col. ill. ;   cm.
Summary: Realistic illustrations take readers through various habitats as
they try to figure out what common trait is shared by a group of animals.
A science and nature book for curious minds.
ISBN 1-56397-988-8
1. Animals, ecology — Juvenile literature. 2. Habitat (Ecology) —
Juvenile literature. (1. Animals, ecology. 2. Habitat (Ecology).)
I. Nadel, Marc, ill. II. Title.
590 21 2002 AC   CIP
2001091726

First edition, 2002
The text of this book is set in 11-point Helvetica.

10 9 8 7 6 5 4 3 2 1

BEASTLY BEHAVIORS

AH, THERE YOU ARE! Glad you could join us as we set off on another fascinating journey into the wonderful world of wildlife.

On each page, we'll come across a diverse range of real animals, from high-flying birds to bottom-dwelling squids. It's our job to search for and identify a common characteristic shared by all the animals in each group. All the animals on one page might be plant eaters, or they might all be able to breathe underwater, or maybe they share something else entirely. Whatever that thing is, it's sure to be amazing!

All the animals you will read about in this book are real. They can be found in the wild, though in some cases, the animals have become very rare. Many are endangered due to factors such as hunting, poaching, and the encroachment of man into their natural habitats.

The best way to approach this assignment is to pay close attention as you read each animal's description of itself. Along with reading, be sure to look at the picture of each animal for clues that may help you figure out what each group has in common. If you get stuck, the answers are provided on the last page of this journal.

As always, it's a good idea to enter these jungle pages quietly, respecting the animals who live here. So grab your gear and let's roll. The first group of critters is waiting just around the page.

Get in the swim of things by identifying what these creatures have in common.

Swamp Rabbit

Hey, y'all! Let's jump in amongst the cane or aquatic plants for some good eating. Then we'll go for a swim. If any predators come a-sniffing around, we can hide with just our noses sticking above the water. But if you don't want to hide, I can stand on my back legs to fight off other rabbits or jump straight off the ground to strike out with my claws.

White-Capped Dipper

I like to jump into a river or shallow stream and walk along the bottom as I eat small fish, tadpoles, and other creatures. I use my stout claws to hang on to the riverbed so I don't get swept away by the current. I like water so much that I usually know how to swim before I can fly. Even my nest is built over water, with the entrance pointing downward.

Chinstrap Penguin

You'll know me by the thin black line across my throat. I'm great in the water, where I can dive down or swim straight along to catch krill and fish. I can even leap up to three feet in order to get out of the water onto the ice. On land, I often drop onto my stomach and toboggan around. I make small circular nests from rocks, just secure enough to keep the eggs from rolling away.

Torrent Duck

Look out below! I love to dive right into all sorts of water, the swifter and wilder the better. I'll grab a bite to eat while I'm in the water, with my feet hanging on to boulders to keep me in place. In fact, my mate and I raise the whole family to be swimmers. We're usually out at dawn or dusk, when insects are most active.

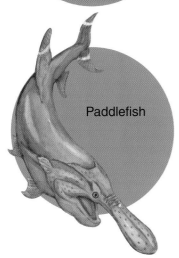

Paddlefish

When people first saw me in the waters of the Mississippi, they thought I was a shark. True, I have a body made of cartilage, not bone, just like a shark, but I'm no meat eater. As I grow older, I lose my teeth to become a filter feeder, which means I swim around with my mouth open, hoping to scoop up very tiny zooplankton. Sensors in my beautiful paddle help me locate these morsels.

Star-Nosed Mole

Mom always said I'd be a star. There are 22 tentacles on my nose, and each is super-sensitive. They are loaded with electro-receptors, like the bill of a platypus or the paddlefish. And it takes a remarkable brain to process the 100,000 nerve fibers that run up from my nose. I'm able to keep my star because I live in wet mud. If I lived in hard, dry ground, the star would get rubbed away as I dug in the dirt.

Japanese Macaque

On the islands where I live, we're in the water a lot. We wash some of our food, and we take baths to warm up. That's because this island is so far north the air gets quite cold. But the volcanic heat from the earth keeps the water warm.

Sitatunga

Call me twinkle-toes! I've got a wide-splayed foot that helps me move quickly through the African swamps. You may notice my back legs are longer than my front ones. My foot joints are so loose that I actually walk on the bones. It doesn't hurt unless I'm on dry land. My water-repellent fur doesn't have much scent, which makes me hard to track.

I spy with my little eye some very interesting animals.

Parotia Bird of Paradise

You may think my feathers look weird, but the girls really go for them. In fact, one reason most male birds have such colorful feathers is to attract a female. We also do a dance to get noticed. Each different species of birds of paradise has its own unique dance.

Pygmy Owl

All I need is a little respect. Even fully grown, I'm only six inches long and weigh less than three ounces! I live in trees or cacti, taking advantage of natural holes or those left by woodpeckers, and I don't add any extra lining to my nest. I can live in a variety of climates, from desert scrub lands to areas alongside waterways.

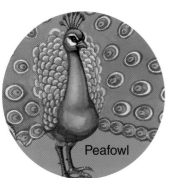

Peafowl

You probably know me as a peacock. I am actually a peafowl, with the male being called a peacock and the female a peahen. Only males have these magnificent feathers with their unique design. In an average train, there are more than 200 individual feathers. I don't stray much in captivity, but I do need a lot of room to walk around. I can fly fairly well, too, so watch out below.

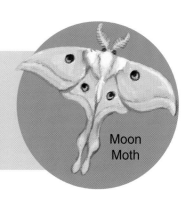

Moon Moth

Hey, something smells around here. Actually, it might not be right around here, since I can smell things more than three miles away. But don't worry, I'll track down where it is. I have one of the most acute senses of smell in nature and can follow a smell better than a Bloodhound. Some other things you might notice are my feathery antennae and the long tails on my hind wings.

Owl Butterfly

I know the coloring of my underside must work because that little Owl guy just invited me out for some foraging. But it's not just coloring that's important. The way that my wings form around my head and body resemble an owl's beak. Most of the flying folks who would like to munch on me are afraid of owls, so I try to flash the full look whenever I'm in a spot of trouble.

Hawkmoth Caterpillar

If you want to see a great impression, check this out. When a bird or predator comes after me, I drop my front half off a branch and hold on with my back legs. Then I inflate my thorax to reveal what looks like the head of a snake. Now, with a little careful moving back and forth, everyone thinks I'm a snake! Ssssimply sssuper!

Four-Eye Butterfly Fish

Here's looking at you, kid, even though you can't tell which way I'm looking. Those spots on my tail help me fool any predators who can't tell which way I'm heading. When they make a lunge at where they think I'm facing, I dart the other way.

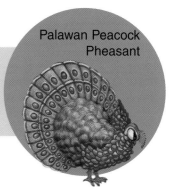

Palawan Peacock Pheasant

Local natives know me as the Tandikan. My species lives on only one tiny island in the whole world, on the floor level of a dwindling forest. As that tiny island in the Philippines becomes more developed, there's less space for us to live. Luckily, I adapt well in confinement.

Be they ever so humble, each of these animals shares a common homey touch.

Mountain Gorilla

Ah, it's so nice to have just a few moments of repose. After all, gorillas are constantly on the move. We continually go back and forth across our domain, eating leaves and moving on. This helps the environment because we don't strip any one area bare and plants have time to regrow. We bend the branches and foliage in order to make a comfortable new spot to rest each night.

Roseate Spoonbill

Everything's rosy when you're a spoonbill. The family and I just flew up from South America, and, boy, are we tired! Our nests are usually about ten to twelve feet off the ground, in colonies with ibises, herons, and egrets. The shape of my bill helps me scoop fish and crustaceans from shallow water. Gotta fly. It's my turn to sit on the egg for a while.

Red-Capped Pygmy Parrot

When I'm wandering through the trees, I love to dig right in. Like a woodpecker, I go after ants and termites. The hard tips of my tail dig into the bark to help keep me steady while I look for insects. Why, I even make my own nest right on top of insect nests in trees. That way I have plenty of food. I'm very quiet and hard to spot.

Red Panda

The black-and-whites and I are distant cousins. I also live in the bamboo forests of the Himalayas, where it's moist and cool. My heavy fur is good in the cold, and I'm sensitive to heat. My specialized hands and claws help me grab and eat the bamboo shoots I love. I prefer to sleep on a branch in a nest, with my legs and arms hanging over the sides and my tail holding me in place.

Horned Guan

How do you like my hat? This red horn is made of skin and bone, not feathers or hair. It's fairly easy to spot as I jump or tiptoe through the high branches. I prefer starting up high because I can glide down from there without having to flap my wings too many times. I sometimes hang upside down like a bat while I eat flowers and fruit.

Lesser Bush Baby

Do I look all right? We spend a great deal of time grooming before we go out. After all, we want to look our best when we're pouncing on insects in the trees. We have great night vision to see the bugs or lizards we eat. During the day, we sleep in the hollows of trees and branches. Our prime nests are only used by the youngsters to catch a nap while the parents are out hunting.

Marbled Murrelet

I prefer to make very simple nests in mossy, old trees. This is a problem because most logging clears out these old trees. When it's not one of those rare moments that I'm in trees, I prefer the water. I'm a good swimmer and diver. I can stroke with my wings, using my feet for steering. I can even catch and swallow fish underwater.

White-Lipped Frog

Most frogs in my family lay their eggs on land, but right from birth I was in a lather. That's because my folks found a patch of ground to make a nest of spit and saliva, which they whipped into a big, foamy pile. Then they laid their eggs in the liquefied center. When it rained, I was able to swim out into a nearby river.

We hope you don't get a big head or an inflated ego once you identify what members of this group have in common.

Bearded Dragon

My beard might look weird, but there's no hair there. My throat pouch is covered with spiky, modified scales. It's all part of the skin I'm in, which I can shed sometimes, like a snake. I use a lot of body language to get my messages across, like bobbing and weaving. I'm fast on all four feet when I need to get moving.

Porcupine Fish

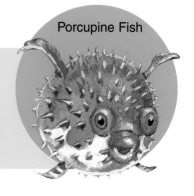

Just like land porcupines, my hard "quills" keep predators away. Not only are they tough to swallow, but I've got some poisons in there. My quills aren't always hard, and I'm not always fat. When threatened, I suck in water, which bloats me. As I expand, my quills stand up. One of the things I eat is coral. I crunch down on the hard rock, grind it in my gullet, and digest the animals living there.

Hooded Seal

I wouldn't stick my big nose in here, but that's what it's there for. Actually, I can puff up twice as much as anyone else. As a male, I can expand my nasal cavity to form the big black ball-like thing you see, but I also have a second, red nasal sac that comes out when I'm feeling aggressive! I don't have many enemies out in the Arctic waters, other than humans or killer whales.

Mexican Burrowing Toad

I love getting down and dirty. My big, flat spadelike feet make it easy for me to push dirt out of the way so I can burrow down to where the ants and termites are working. Then I stick out my rodlike tongue and enjoy the buffet. When I can't hide from somebody, I take a deep breath to inflate myself and look more impressive. Can you dig it?

Speke's Gazelle

Ah-choo! Sorry, but I may have caught a cold standing near the seal. It's usually much warmer at home in Africa. My loud sneeze is formed in the expandable nasal sac that I can inflate to the size of a golf ball. One of the ways I use that sound is as an alarm that danger is approaching. As one of the smaller members of the gazelle family, I've developed a real nose for trouble.

Magnificent Frigate Bird

How magnificent I am! I have a huge chest and a wingspan of more than six feet. When a bird is flying home with a mouth full of food, I fly along to bother it until it coughs up its food. Then I dive to catch the food before it hits the water. I don't like water much because my feathers are not waterproof.

Plains Spadefoot

I may not be a big shot, but I do all right for my size. And though my smoother skin makes me look like a frog, I'm a toad and proud of it. While others may have to burrow in, I can dig straight down. My feet have hard spadelike edges that let me push the dirt away from beneath me. I can actually "sink" right where I am.

Umbrella Bird

Well, hey there! I can raise my brow and raise the roof. Once I've got my humming call amplified through these inflatable wattles hanging on my chin, it really gets the ladies shaking and quaking in their tail feathers. After a light supper of mostly fruit, I call it a day.

If ever you need a hand, someone in this group is sure to have one free to lend.

Binturong

Most call me Bear Cat because I look like a little of each. I act like other animals as well. I climb down trees headfirst like a squirrel; I can balance on my back feet and tail like a kangaroo; I walk flat-footed like a bear, not just on the front part of my feet; and I can release a strong-smelling spray like a skunk. My long fur is thick and rain-repellent, and my saliva is medicinal for humans. You could say I've got it all!

Howler Monkey

HEY! LISTEN UP! I'll try to whisper, but they don't call me howler for nothing. I'm the loudest land animal, and my calls can be heard up to three miles away. Only the blue whale has a louder call. My call has evolved to be so impressive because we males get into howling matches to set the boundaries for our troops. My tail is so strong that if I fall out of a tree, I can use my tail to catch a branch.

Parson's Chameleon

You must be green with envy to see me! Well, I've been other colors, too. People aren't sure why I can change colors. Some think it's defensive, so I can blend into the background. Others think I change in response to the light and temperature. Each of my eyes can rotate independently so I can see all around in a complete circle, without even moving my head. I actually prefer not to move at all for long periods.

Spotted Cuscus

If I look clumsy, it's because I'm all thumbs. Actually, I've got two on each hand. They're great for climbing and getting around in the trees, especially at night, when you need that extra grip. My pouch, which I use to carry my babies, and a prehensile tail are other great additions that help keep my hands free.

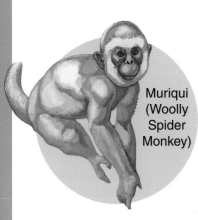

Muriqui (Woolly Spider Monkey)

That Howler may think he's big, but I'm the largest primate in South America. I also happen to be one of the world's rarest mammals. And though I don't have any thumbs, I can swing through the trees, climb, run on all fours, or even stand up straight. I'm not very aggressive, and prefer to throw nuts and twigs at my enemies.

Kinkajou

If you can see me, you might call me Honey Bear or Night Walker. I'm very fast, and I'm a fairly agile jumper. You may get a glimpse of my tail, which is often longer than my body. I live my whole life in trees, often hanging upside down to pluck fruit from branches. Though I'm usually a quiet sort, I do have a sharp bite and sharp claws.

Cave Salamander

Know what spelunking is? It's climbing around and exploring caves. It's what I love to do. I climb all over the walls, looking for moist spots under rocks and ledges. While I live mainly near a cave's mouth, European cave salamanders prefer the deeper, darker parts. Since they never see light, many are born blind, with skin over their eyes.

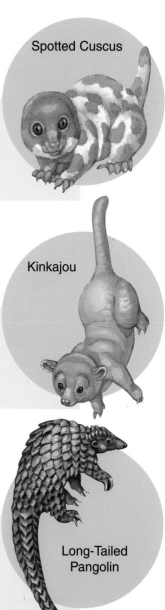

Long-Tailed Pangolin

Whenever a predator threatens, I roll into an impenetrable ball, with the sharp edges of my scales sticking out. These scales are really tough, cemented hair, like a rhino's horn. My extra-long tongue can stick out to 25 centimeters, which helps me lick up my food. Because my strong claws are so big and curved, I have to walk on my knuckles.

Pull up a box, and you can be instrumental in discovering what this lot has in common. You'll get a handle on it in no time.

Woodpecker Finch

Though I get my name from a bird with a long tongue, I have only a short one. And I have the short beak of a finch. I wish I had the longer woodpecker beak to reach the insects and larvae that I love to eat. But I do okay by ripping off the old bark from trees and using a twig or cactus spine to root out a few tasty morsels.

Satin Bowerbird

When I'm blue, it's because I'm happy! I love the color blue. Why, I even paint things to make them blue. To attract a female, I build a bower on the ground. A bower is like a small room, though mine is made from grass, leaves, and whatever else I find. If the place still needs a little something, I chew up berries and charcoal to make a blue paint. Then I use a piece of bark to splatter the "paint" all over the walls.

Sea Otter

I do everything in the water. Eating, sleeping, even raising my pup are all done in the water. To sleep, I use a strand of kelp to hold me in place; then I cover my eyes with my paws. I'm the smallest of all sea mammals. Luckily, my fur is superdense, with up to 650,000 hairs per square inch. I rely on the natural oils in my fur to repel water and to trap tiny air bubbles that keep me warm.

Noisy Pitta

The Aborigines of Australia called me the Devil-Devil Bird because they believed my bright colors and friendly calls would lure children to run off into the woods. But I'm only after snails. I bang the shell on a stone until it shatters and then eat the goodies inside.

Long-Tailed Tailorbird

To build a nest, we first find some good leaves and then poke holes along the edges. Next, we find a spider web, plant fibers, or grass to pull through the holes. Then we have to knot the grass and hope it all holds. Finally, we stuff the pouch full of grass or animal hair to make it warm. That's a lot to accomplish in three or four days. But all that flitting about helps pollinate plants, so we work in a good cause.

Peter's Tent-Making Bat

Many bats live in shelters made by humans, but I prefer my own space. A couple of strategic bites along the veins of certain leaves make them fold over into quite a nice shelter that can last up to a year. Sometimes it takes more than one leaf to get it right. These tents shelter us from rain or sun but still let us look out for snakes and other predators.

Chimpanzee

Chimps are the most humanlike of animals. We use facial expressions, vocalizations, body language, grooming, kisses, and pats to communicate. We suffer from many human diseases, including colds, flu, and malaria; and we eat wild medicinal plants that help treat some of these ills. We can use a twig to remove ants from an anthill. We learn quickly by watching others, so be careful what you do around us.

Acorn Woodpecker

You might think I'm nuts, but I love acorns. I stuff them into holes in tree branches and bark in case food gets scarce. I prefer to eat things in treetops, like insects and fruit, and rarely come to the ground. Another big treat is sucking sap with a flock of friends. We share the same holes to drink, and we're quite noisy when we get together.

Hope you've got a good light to read by because it is dark in here. Even so, it shouldn't take all day to spot what these creatures have in common.

Avahi (Woolly Lemur)

I like hanging around but can jump when the need arises. I'm a vertical leaper (which means straight up), and my legs are so strong I don't even use my feet for propulsion. In the trees I use my arms and legs, but on the ground I get by on two feet. I can use my tail to balance or to send signals to other lemurs.

Long-Eared Owl

You might think these big tufts are my ears, but they're just feathers. My ears are actually tiny holes hidden on the side of my head, but I have excellent hearing. Even the feathers on my face are designed to funnel sound directly to my ears. I can turn my head up to 3/4 of a circle around to make sure my ears face what I want to hear.

Tapir

Tapirs were on earth even before people, more than 35 million years ago. I'm actually related to the rhino and the horse. I'm a very good swimmer and can walk along the bottoms of rivers and ponds. With a nose like this, you know I've got a keen sense of smell. I can also use my snout to pull at the vegetation I eat, the way an elephant uses its trunk.

Mexican Long-Nosed Bat

My nose is nothing to sniff at. It helps me locate and get at the nectar and pollen in flowers. I also have a magnificent tongue that can dart up to three inches, which is the average length of my body. I can be found in hollow trees, mines, rock piles, and caves, with up to 150 individuals packed in per square foot.

Desert Pocket Mouse

During the heat of the day, I close the entrance to my burrow and dig through the hardened crust of soil to get down to where things are cooler. I stay active at night. I go out to get a nice selection of seeds and grasses, pack them in my cheek pouches, and head back to the burrow for some more relaxing.

Angwantibo (Golden Potto)

Is it hot in here? I'm so sensitive to heat that I try to stay in the moist middle branches of Africa's rain forests. My body continuously eliminates fluids, making me susceptible to dehydration. I sniff out the insects that make up most of my diet. I can even rear up on my hind legs to grab moths in flight. If I bump into anyone unfriendly, I stand on my long legs and slash with claws and teeth.

Clouded Leopard

Other leopards have clear rosettes on their coats, but mine are a bit fuzzy. I have great hearing, terrific eyesight, and a sharp sense of smell. I have no trouble putting the bite on dinner because I have the largest upper canine teeth in relation to body size of any big cat. I climb well and sometimes drag my prey up into tree branches for an undisturbed snack.

Feather Tail Glider

Let me tell you a tale of my tail! It's fringed with stiff hair, like a feather, and helps me navigate when gliding in the dark from tree to tree. But I can also use it to hang on to things. And when I want to come in for a landing, my toes have large pads that help me grip smooth surfaces. Why do I do all this gliding? In search of food, of course, like insects, larvae, nectar, seeds, and my favorite—grapes!

Shh. Be very quiet as you read through these descriptions. We don't want to disturb anyone as we try to figure out what they all have in common.

Gray Lesser
Mouse Lemur

Thank you for whispering. My large membranous ears are very sensitive and can pick up noises from far away. This helps me look for something to eat while also helping me to keep from being eaten. I'd invite you over for dinner, but I don't think we eat the same things. One delicacy I like is insect larvae on tree branches.

Poorwill

I got my name from my very loud call, which sounds exactly as if I'm saying "Poor Will." Some people call me a whippoorwill. My small feet make it hard for me to hop on the ground. That's why I prefer to fly. I live throughout all the United States and Canada but like to spend winters in California and Mexico.

Woodchuck

I may look like a chubby chucker, but I'm a good climber, swimmer, and digger. I make burrows that have front doors as well as escape tunnels. My burrowing work is so well known that my abandoned holes are used by rabbits, foxes, and other small animals. Some call me a groundhog, while others call me a whistle pig!

Glacier Bear

My name comes from the bluish icy tint of my fur, which blends into the Alaskan environment. Since the environment has changed, glacier bears are very rare now. When I was born, I weighed only one pound and looked like a small rat. As an adult, I can weigh more than a thousand pounds, thanks to a diet of fish, small mammals, and berries. I need to pack on those pounds to hold me over while I hibernate.

Arctic Ground
Squirrel

Do the "Tundra glide"! Just keep low to the ground and sort of slide from place to place. It sounds like a dance, but I do it to keep out of sight from flying predators. The Inuit people where I live call me "sik-sik" for the noise I make. Besides looking for food up to 17 hours a day, I like to sunbathe, sandbathe, and swim. Of the thing that all the animals on this page have in common, I do it the longest.

Peacock Butterfly

"Eye" see you. Can you see me? The eyes really have it when it comes to my markings. But they are there for more than just to look good, darlings. When a predator comes near, I flash my wings open to resemble an owl's face. That, plus the noise I make by rubbing my wings together, will usually scare off any trespassers.

Eastern Pipistrelle

You might say I'm a pip-squeak. Pip is part of my name, and my call is a high-pitched squeak. I'm also the smallest of all bats in the eastern U.S. If I appear to have a "sparkling" personality, that's because while I sleep, water droplets cover my body. The droplets drip down as condensation from the roofs of the mines that I roost in.

Pale Kangaroo
Mouse

Oh, I feel a little faint. My name comes more from the shape of my tail than from any bouncing abilities. I prefer to get around on all four legs rather than hop about on two. The shape of my tail allows me to store nutrients that I can use for energy. When I have to bounce, the tail is a big help in keeping my balance.

Don't let this group of weird wildlife egg you on. Take your time, and once you've read their descriptions, you should have the lay of the land.

Platypus

G'day! I've got a beaver's tail, webbed feet, and a venomous spur on the back of my feet. And I'm very sensitive about my nose. It may look hard, like a duck's bill, but it's actually covered with soft skin that has many nerve endings. When I hatched, I didn't even have this bill, just elongated lips. Otherwise, I never would have gotten enough milk to grow into such a handsome specimen.

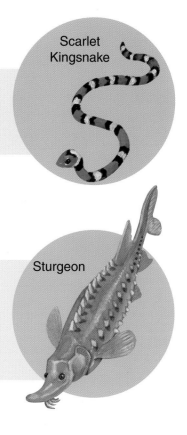

Scarlet Kingsnake

Sssshh! I'm in disguise. Many people think I'm the venomous Eastern Coral Snake. Actually, I'm harmless to humans but not to other snakes and small rodents. I put the squeeze on those characters to get something to eat. My eggs are laid in a clutch that I make in the forest floor.

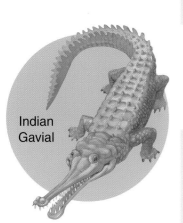

Indian Gavial

Just look at my beautiful snout. It's got more than 100 teeth and has no lips to keep the water out. It's especially thin, so I can move it quickly in the water, whether I'm going straight ahead or need to whisk it to the side to snap up a passing morsel. One bad thing is that I can't lift my belly off the ground. When I move, it's a real drag.

Sturgeon

Somebody call for a doctor? I always wanted to be a doctor. I even went to school for it. Get it? That's an old joke, but what do you expect from a fish that's been around since prehistoric times. If I live to be 100—and some of us do—I might not have any teeth, but these barbs at the end of my nose help me get plenty to eat. Humans take my eggs to make caviar. That's pretty rich, huh?

Bee Hummingbird

¡Hola, Amigo! You may have trouble seeing me since I'm the smallest living bird in the world. I'm just two inches fully grown, more than half of which is my bill. In the tropics, there is lots of sun and warm air, which help the flowers that give me the nectar I need to move and live. Nectar gives me energy to flap my wings up to 200 times a second. That allows me to fly like a helicopter—up, down, or even backward.

Asian Giant Softshell Turtle

I can stay underwater a long time because I have a special pharynx in my throat that lets me take oxygen out of the water. I'm an old softie because my shell doesn't form into hard plates. When I lay eggs, I usually don't lay them all at once. I'll put up to 27 or so in one nest and then move to another spot to lay more.

Knob-Tailed Gecko

I can walk straight up a wall or tree, thanks to my special feet. The toes have very soft skin, with little indents like suction cups. I've also got tiny hairs around my toes that have hooks on them. These hairs act like Velcro and help me cling to almost any surface. If a predator puts the bite on me, I'll disconnect my tail and run away, leaving him holding the still-twitching end.

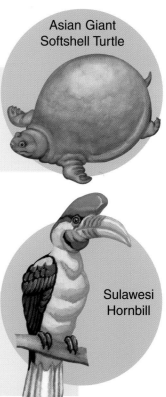

Sulawesi Hornbill

Hornbills nest in a hole in a tree. When the female goes inside the hole, I use mud to wall up the front of the hole until I can stick in only my beak. I bring food that I push into her beak while she sits with the eggs. Once the kids are born, she breaks out. We then block the kids back in, keeping them safe until they're ready to fly.

You should have what these critters have in common in the bag in no time.

Great Gray Marsupial Frog

I'm one of the few frogs whose babies emerge fully grown, not as tadpoles. I carry the eggs under a protective cover on my back, where they are nourished by the yolks and wrapped in their own gills. When the froglets push out, they can be jumping on their own within ten seconds! Those kids really keep me hopping here in South America.

Quokka

My unusual name comes from the Aboriginal people here in Australia. Once plentiful, I can now be found mainly on two small islands. Though I may look like a big rat, I'm really related to kangaroos and wallabies. I hop some but prefer to run through tunnels and runways I create in the tall grass.

Pretty Faced Wallaby

Wallabies are the smaller relatives of the kangaroo family. We normally have feet that are less than ten inches long. That's just one way to tell the difference. I'm very sociable, living in mobs of around 50. My distinctive cheek markings are what make me so pretty. Another name I may go by is the Whiptail Wallaby.

Tasmanian Devil

I know you're disappointed that I'm not spinning and growling. Sorry, I'm not a good climber or runner, either. And I often prefer to use my sharp teeth and strong jaws on carrion rather than attack a live animal. The pouch for my young opens to the rear, so the youngsters have to do quite a bit of maneuvering if they want a ride.

Greater Flying Possum

I'm not flying now, but I actually have arm flaps to glide along on air currents. The flaps stretch out from my body, running from my arms to my legs. Although I can climb very well, it's really a big help to be able to "fly" from tree to tree. I've been known to travel more than 110 meters in one glide.

Water Opossum (Yapok)

I'm the only marsupial who's fully adapted to aquatic life, spending most of my time in small streams and rivers in South America. Even my burrow is in a riverbank, with the opening above the water line but the den itself below. Both the males and females in my family have pouches. The female's pouches can be tightened enough to keep her young dry while she's swimming.

Most bandicoots nest above ground. I'm the only branch of my family that lives in burrows, highly specialized for desert living. Though I live alone, my burrow can be quite long and complex. I require very little water, and though I sometimes eat plants, I prefer insects and small animals. My hair is also different, since it is much smoother and silkier than the usual spiky fur of most bandicoots.

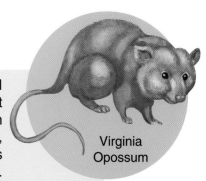

Virginia Opossum

I'm the only marsupial native to North America. When I was born, I made a trail up my mother's stomach to her pouch. I'm active at night all year long, and I can carry some material with my tail. I can be very vicious in a fight, but often I'll just stand still, not blinking, with my tongue hanging out, pretending to be dead. Whatever is after me usually gets confused and goes away.

Rabbit-Eared Bandicoot (Bilby)

See if you can dig up enough clues to guess what we have in common.

Mountain Crab

Though my name may sound lofty, I really prefer to lie low. I like digging in the sand, in low-lying areas at a beach. That way, I can surprise my dinner if it comes walking by. Plus, with some good seaside property, I can always jump in the water to cool off.

Oldfield Mouse

I'm an explosive little guy who loves to spend time at the beach. I build long tunnels, which I sometimes plug up to keep out nosy predators. But when one comes sniffing along, I can push behind the plug to explode right out. I usually get past the predator while he's trying to figure out what just happened.

Blue-Tailed Mole Skink

I can swim through sand. I spend most of my time about two inches below the surface of the sand, and my body is so sleek that I just slide between the grains. Many skinks start out with blue tails but lose them as they mature. My family manages to hold on to the coloring well into old age, which for a skink may be only a few years.

Marsupial Mole

I can't swim underground like some, but I move pretty well. My compact body is so sleek that my ears are hidden under the skin. I'm blind, which is okay. Underground everything is right in my face when I need to find it. Check out my nose, and you'll see that I've got a "shield" on it. That's so I can keep digging without bruising it. I seldom need to drink since I get moisture from the grubs I eat.

Fennec Fox

Pretty silly-looking ears, huh? Well, if you laugh, I'll hear you because I can pick up the slightest sounds, even from a distance. I have the largest ears in relation to body size of any member of the fox family. They also help radiate the heat out of my body so I don't overheat. I can go a long time without water, which is helpful when you live in the desert.

I'm the smallest of all North American swallows, so some people don't notice me. But they sure notice my nest. I live in colonies of hundreds of birds, and we can make a riverbank or a sea cliff look like a piece of Swiss cheese. If a bigger bird, like a starling or sparrow, comes along, it might force me out of one nest, so I'd have to dig another. But I'd be chipping away with my beak in no time. You can bank on that!

Bank Swallow

Sewellel (Mountain Beaver)

Life is just sewellel when you're a good digger, good swimmer, and a pretty fair climber. Of course, I've had a long time to practice all these skills since my family members are probably the oldest living rodents on earth. One big problem I have is the need for a cool, stable climate, since I can't regulate my own body temperature.

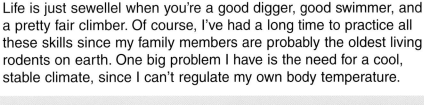

I don't live in the water all the time, unlike my cousin the Sea Otter. Still, I like a good swim—or a run, or a wrestling match. But a good slide is best. I run a little bit and then throw myself forward to slide a short way in mud or snow. My fur is short but very thick, which insulates me from the cold. In summer, the openings to my den are above the water. In winter, I close the top and only use the underwater entrance.

River Otter

Let the information ooze into your brain before you shoot out any answer about what the members of this group have in common.

Zorilla

When you first saw me, I bet you thought I was a skunk. Well, I'm more closely related to a weasel. However, like a skunk, I can spray a very smelly spray when somebody comes too close. I'm also carnivorous and nocturnal. I live in the African savannahs. I'm a fine swimmer and can even climb trees if I have to get at my food.

I hope my spikes look tough because I'm actually quite timid. If I see someone coming to eat me, I flatten and freeze. My coloring lets me blend with the ground, and I flatten so I don't throw a shadow. If I do get into a confrontation, I can shoot blood from my eyes, which is sure to ward off most predators.

Horned Lizard

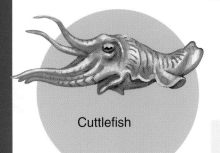

Cuttlefish

What animal can change its body color faster than a chameleon, has three hearts and blue blood, is jet-propelled, can squirt inkscreens, and is among the most intelligent of all invertebrates? Hope you guessed me! Actually, all cephalopods have these characteristics. Like squids, I have a shell that is internal. It's this cuttlebone that helps me control my buoyancy as I float.

Ready, aim, fire! I'm the world's best water blaster. When I press my tongue against the long groove in my mouth and then compress my gill covers, I can spit out a drop of water capable of knocking an insect off a branch. I usually hit what I'm aiming at because my excellent eyes compensate for the refraction of the water.

Archerfish

European Fire Salamander

The "fire" in my name doesn't come from the poisonous toxin that I can shoot out at predators but from the fact that I like to hide in shady crevices or logs. When ancient people threw some of those logs on a fire, my ancestors would skedaddle before they burned. When we ran out of the fire, people thought we lived in the actual flames!

I may look like just a bug, but I'm really a chemical genius. I carry four different kinds of chemicals inside my body. Some of these chemicals are meant to keep the others from mixing together. That's because when I squeeze my sacs together and mix them up, there's a bang! A boiling hot spray shoots out to splash whoever may be bothering me.

Bombardier Beetle

Spitting Cobra

Like other cobras, I can form a hood when I'm excited. That's the first warning to back off. If you don't listen, I will spit venom while you're still a few feet away. I usually aim for the eyes when I spit. My venom can cause temporary eye damage. If you keep coming, I'll have to put the bite on you. My bites are very dangerous and may require amputation of a bitten limb.

Shining Tube-Shoulder Fish

I'm sure you can see me since I glow in the dark. I've got so much light going on inside me I sometimes squirt it out through the tubes on my shoulders. This kind of natural light is called bioluminescence. I use it to counter-illuminate the area where I'm swimming so that a predator won't be able to pick me out from the surrounding area. I get some of the ability to do this from nutrients in the shrimp I love to eat.

Let your imagination fly as you look through these friendly fowl. Sure, they are all birds, but what else do they have in common?

Kiwi

Kiwis have good eyesight and good hearing. If you had been a predator, I would have run away on my muscular legs. One wild thing you might pick out on me is my nostrils. They're way down at the end of my bill, not close up to my face. I have sensitive bristles along my nose that help me look for food. I'm so popular in my native New Zealand that people here refer to themselves as Kiwis.

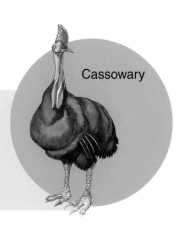
Cassowary

As the largest land creature in New Guinea, I stand above other animals. If one of them tries to push me around, I usually run. But I can defend myself by kicking. My feet have claws and a long nail on the innermost of my three toes. I really use my head when looking for food. That bony piece helps me move the dirt around until I can find some grub.

Macaroni Penguin

Come on in, the water's fine. Our "wings" evolved for flapping, and our tails act like rudders. I'm extremely sociable and love to be in big groups. We penguins stay warm because our thick feathers trap in layers of air, and we have deposits of fat that keep the cold from reaching our bones. Got to hop to it because that's how I get around.

Steamer Duck

Whoa, look out! People call me a steamer because of the way I pump my legs and wings to run across the top of water. I look like an old paddle-wheel steamboat. I lay from six to twelve eggs, but only one egg per day. But the great thing is, all the eggs usually hatch on the same day. How's that for planning?

Takahe

I'm back! For a while, people thought I was extinct. But then a small group of us came out of hiding. Still, we don't have it easy because we don't fly to escape predators. I eat seeds from grass that I tear up in my strong bill. Unfortunately, the expansion of building is wiping out the grass and seeds I need.

King Penguin

Hello, loyal subjects. We kings are the second largest of all penguins. The emperor is larger, while we look trimmer and have sharper bills. Though we may stumble about a bit on land, in the water we can swim faster than most birds can fly. We also can see better in the water than on land. As for future generations, we incubate the little eggs by holding them on our feet.

Okinawa Rail

The saying "thin as a rail" originated from people looking at our thin, compressed bodies. It pays to stay in shape because that helps us move through the dense vegetation. We like to roost in the very low branches of trees. This keeps us close to the ground so we can jump down in case of attack.

Rhea

I come from a "big" family. Along with the ostrich and the emu, we're some of the largest birds ever. At five feet in height, we're the largest bird in all the Americas. Even our eggs are big. In volume, it would take twelve chicken eggs to fill one rhea egg. But all this size has a drawback, since our wings are too small to get us off the ground.

You may think we're pretty, but we each share a potent secret. Can you figure out what it is?

Mexican Beaded Lizard

I may look like a Gila Monster, but my skin is bumpier, and I'm usually larger. But like the Gila, I have powerful jaws with venomous glands and sharp teeth that can lock on for a good bite. I rarely attack humans unless they bother me. I hiss to let them know when I'm angry. Otherwise, I prefer to eat rodents and the eggs of ground-dwelling birds.

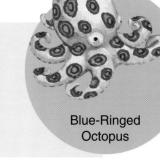

Blue-Ringed Octopus

Normally, I'm quite happy to remain hard to see in plain brown and yellow. But when I'm agitated my rings turn bright blue. Though small, I can do a lot of damage. I have a powerful poison that causes breathing failure, and there is no known antivenin. I can bite a human, or I can spit the poison through the water onto crabs, which are my favorite food. Once they're stunned and can't move, I put the arm on them for a quick meal.

Lionfish

When I'm hungry, my friends and I hunt in packs like lions. I don't eat anything larger than a small fish, though. My quills can be very dangerous. Stepping on one of my quills or touching one can give you a very bad wound, though it's rarely fatal. I carry my eggs around inside my body until they hatch and are ready to swim on their own. This helps protect my young from other predators.

Poison-Dart Frog

As a frog, you might think I spend a lot of time in the water. Wrong! I seldom go to water pools except to reproduce. I'm arboreal, which means I spend my time in trees that I climb using the adhering disks at the end of my fingers. My body contains more than 300 different chemicals, some of which may be useful as medicines.

Hooded Pitohui

The natives of New Guinea call me the Rubbish Bird, partly due to the poor taste of my skin. Believe it or not, I fall into the songbird category. Unlike most bird species, both the females and the males of my family have colorful feathers. I use my special abilities only to protect myself from predators, never to attack anyone.

Gaboon Viper

You might think I've got a big mouth, and I do! First, I can open my mouth almost a full 180 degrees, with my fangs extended outward. Second, I have very flexible jawbones, which allow me to open my mouth enough to swallow whatever animals I kill. I may look scary, but I'm not very aggressive. I only bite when forced into a corner.

Bark Scorpion

All these animals are youngsters! My family's been around for more than 450 million years. I'm such a strong survivor, I can go up to 500 days without food. But when I'm hungry, look out! I'll eat any sort of bug that crosses my path, including other scorpions. But eating's no picnic, since I have to use my digestive juices to break down my prey into an edible soft mass.

American Short-Tailed Shrew

My high metabolism keeps me on the go. My family is always in a state of manic rage. I'm very aggressive, constantly swallowing food. If I'm forced to be without food for more than two hours, I'll even eat other shrews. When I catch my prey, my saliva quickly paralyzes it.

ANSWER KEY

pages 4-5
All these animals are good swimmers and do well in water.

pages 6-7
All these beauties have eye spots as part of their natural coloring.

pages 8-9
All these creatures are nest builders.

pages 10-11
All these animals can inflate parts of their bodies.

pages 12-13
All these beasts have prehensile tails.

pages 14-15
All these animals are tool users.

pages 16-17
All this wildlife is primarily nocturnal.

pages 18-19
All this fauna hibernates for certain periods.

pages 20-21
All these animals lay eggs.

pages 22-23
All these creatures have pouches.

pages 24-25
All these animals dig their burrows.

pages 26-27
All these animals can shoot or spray something from their bodies.

pages 28-29
All these birds are unable to fly.

pages 30-31
All these animals are poisonous or venomous.